Princess Pumpkin Patch

Written by Andi Cann

Illustrated by Elena Schweitzer

I hope you enjoy learning about Princess Pumpkin Patch today! Please visit my website https://www.andicann.com and register your email address. You will receive a free book and be the first to know about new books, special offers, and free stuff!

If you have a chance, please write a review. It helps other readers and me, an independent author. Thank you!

Andi

To my parents. Thank you for

believing in me.

Once upon a time, there was a beautiful butterfly castle.

Surrounding the castle were thousands and thousands

of pumpkins. All of the pumpkins in the world grew in

the Pumpkin Patch Kingdom.

At that time pumpkins were square, not round, like they are today.

Her Royal Majesty, Princess Sassinia Pumpkin Patch, ruled the Kingdom. She was called "Sassi" by her friends. You may call her Sassi, too.

The Pumpkin Princess was in charge of the pumpkin harvest every year and did a fine job, indeed.

The pumpkins were harvested and sent around the world. Because of Sassi, we have Halloween pumpkins, pumpkin pies, and delicious pumpkin bread.

When the harvest was over, Princess Pumpkin Patch

had a wonderful life. Every day was like her birthday!

She loved winter especially, and wandered the hills and forests with her dog, Pandy, delivering bread to the villagers, and enjoying the cold, snowy air.

The village people loved and admired the princess.

They expected her to be their pumpkin harvest leader

forever. But the princess felt like something was

missing.

She had a nagging feeling she should be doing more.

She didn't feel like harvesting pumpkins was quite

"enough" for her. Was she making a difference? Was

she doing enough?

People tried to tell her, "You're wonderful. You're the best pumpkin princess ever."

Hmmm, the princess wondered as she gazed at the village from her bedroom high in the castle. Was life only about sweet treats and pumpkin harvests? What was there beyond the village?

The Princess looked up at her friend Oscar one wintery day and asked, "Oscar, is this all there is? Should I be doing more?"

He considered her question. He knew she needed to find an answer. He said in his most serious and wise voice, "It is almost winter. There is time before the next pumpkin harvest. Go. Discover the world. Seek your answers."

Sassi agreed to go on the journey. Pandy thought it was a great idea, too (even though Pandy could not go with her!) Oscar gave her these instructions: "First, put someone in charge of the kingdom. Then, hold onto a balloon or two or three and go to the very edge of the sky. There you will discover something."

Sassi gave her friend, Felipe, her crown and left him in

charge. "Be kind but fair," she instructed.

Following Oscar's directions, she sailed into the sky holding three balloons.

Soon, she reached the edge of the sky where she discovered it needed help. The inky darkness was fading. Sassi poured more black into the darkness so people could see the stars.

Then, she brightened the stars and hung them in the sky. She felt better helping the sky. But she was still restless. She did not find her answer.

She found an umbrella and continued her search. She even stood in the windy, blowy rain hoping an answer would magically appear.

An answer did not, but Oscar did! Sassi explained she

had not yet found the answer to her questions, "Am I

making a difference? Am I enough?"

Oscar complimented her on her good work with the stars and the sky. Then, he sent her to the sea. She arrived at a castle on the very edge of the stormy sea.

Sassi found a lamp, lit it, and hung it outside. While in the castle she asked the questions, "Do I make a difference? Am I doing enough?"

She looked at the sea but found no answers. Sadly,

she made her way home. As she walked through the

Toadstool forest on the way to the village, she saw

Oscar yet again.

"Hello, Oscar. I have not been able to find my answers," Sassi said sadly.

Oscar encouraged her. "You are getting closer. Look for toadstools in the bright light. You will know where to go when the time is right."

Finally, she saw a snowy Toadstool house with a clock on its front. She went into the home, lit a lantern, and hung it outside.

To her surprise, a book worm appeared and said,

"Hello, My name is Boxmillian. My friends call me

Boxy. I have been in the dark until you came along and

hung the lantern. Thank you!"

Even though she didn't know him very well, Sassi

asked, "Boxy, when will my heart feel full? Will I ever

feel like I have done enough?"

Boxy looked at her and said, "Oh, my dear. You have

journeyed so very far. You traveled over hills and seas

and through seasons and trees. But you have one more

stop to make. Go to the knowledge tree. There you

will find your answer."

Sassi went to the knowledge tree. She saw a door and opened it. Inside, there was someone who looked just like Oscar!

"Hello, Sassinia, I am Noni, Oscar's grandmother." She smiled and asked, "How was your journey? Did you find your answers?"

"How do you know what I've come to ask?" Sassi asked.

"Oscar has been sharing your journey with me. So, my dear, do you have your answer?"

Sassi shook her head, feeling very sad. "I don't. I don't have an answer," she slightly sobbed.

Noni smiled and said gently, "My dear. Think about the

sky. Think about the sea." Princess Sassinia just

shook her head. "Think about the light." Noni

continued, "You, my dear. You are the answer. It is the

light you bring to the world that makes you "enough."

Your heart is so full of love you had light left over to

power the stars. You, my dear, are full of light, of love.

Your beautiful heart is the answer."

Sassi looked surprised. "I don't understand."

Oscar's grandmother went on, "From the castle by the sea to the Toadstool house in the forest, your light shone wherever you went. You lit up every place you went because you are kind, fair, and loving. You are not important simply because you grow and ship pumpkins. You are important because you are you. Wonderful, loving you."

Sassi thought deeply about Noni's words, closed her eyes, and pictured the light inside of her.

She suddenly realized that Noni's words were true.

She was enough. She even felt, dare she say it, special. She suddenly wanted everyone to know they were special, too.

Over the hills and back to her castle, Sassi carried love

in her heart. She saw light and love everywhere.

When she returned to the Kingdom, she issued a decree. For the rest of time, pumpkins would be round, to remind everyone of the sun and the light each person brings to the world!

And so, the story ends with the sweet truth Princess

Pumpkin Patch found. Remember you are light and

love whenever you see a pumpkin that is round.

Thank you for reading and for leaving a review!

Published by MindView Press: Hibou

ANDI CANN
BOOKS FOR KIDS

Made in the USA
Middletown, DE
09 November 2021